Dear Parent:
Your child's love of reading

Every child learns to read in a different way and at his or her own speed. Some go back and forth between reading levels and read favorite books again and again. Others read through each level in order. You can help your young reader improve and become more confident by encouraging his or her own interests and abilities. From books your child reads with you to the first books he or she reads alone, there are I Can Read Books for every stage of reading:

SHARED READING
Basic language, word repetition, and whimsical illustrations, ideal for sharing with your emergent reader

BEGINNING READING
Short sentences, familiar words, and simple concepts for children eager to read on their own

READING WITH HELP
Engaging stories, longer sentences, and language play for developing readers

READING ALONE
Complex plots, challenging vocabulary, and high-interest topics for the independent reader

I Can Read Books have introduced children to the joy of reading since 1957. Featuring award-winning authors and illustrators and a fabulous cast of beloved characters, I Can Read Books set the standard for beginning readers.

A lifetime of discovery begins with the magical words **"I Can Read!"**

Visit www.icanread.com for information
on enriching your child's reading experience.

Baby Shark: Happy Mommy's Day

© The Pinkfong Company. All Rights Reserved. Pinkfong™ Baby Shark™ and Baby Shark's Big Show!™

are trademarks of The Pinkfong Company, registered or pending rights worldwide. © 2023 Viacom

International Inc. All Rights Reserved. Nickelodeon is a trademark of Viacom International Inc.

Printed in the United States of America.

For information address HarperCollins Children's Books, a division of HarperCollins Publishers,

195 Broadway, New York, NY 10007.

www.icanread.com

Library of Congress Control Number: 2022946655

ISBN 978-0-06-315897-9

Book design by Stephanie Hays

23 24 25 26 27 LB   10 9 8 7 6 5 4 3 2 1   First Edition

I Can Read!

BEGINNING READING 1

pinkfong
BABY SHARK™

Happy Mommy's Day

Adapted by Megan Roth

HARPER
An Imprint of HarperCollinsPublishers

nickelodeon

It's Mother's Day!

Baby Shark and his friends

have a plan.

It's called Operation Happy Mommies.

They want to surprise their moms.

Every mom deserves

a great Mother's Day!

Baby Shark is going to make a feast for his mommy and grandma. Hank is going to clean the house for his stepmom.

Vola is going to make seashell art

for her mom and mama.

William will dance with his mom.

"Wait, that's your mom?"
Shadow asks William.
"But she's a manta ray
and you're a pilot fish."

"Well, I was adopted. I had a pilot fish birth mom," William says.

"Then my manta mom took me home."

"It can be hard having a family that doesn't look like everyone else's," William says.

Operation Happy Mommies will help!

Baby Shark starts his plan first.

He and his friends sneak

into his house.

They cook a fantastic feast.

Daddy Shark and Grandpa Shark help.

They yell "Surprise!" when Mommy

Shark and Grandma Shark come home.

Grandma Shark and Mommy Shark

love their surprise.

They take a family photo.

William sees the Shark family photo.

He wonders if families

should look the same.

Hank starts his plan next.

He and his friends clean the house.

His dad helps too.

His stepsisters, Ashley and Splashly,

almost make another mess.

Hank plays hide and hunt with them.

His friends and dad finish cleaning.

"Surprise!" they cheer.

"Happy Mother's Day!"

Hank's stepmom loves her surprise.

She also loves seeing her daughters

playing with Hank.

William notices Hank's family

looks different than his too.

Vola starts her plan next.

She needs a lot of seashells.

Her friends help her find some.

Vola has an inkling

of what she wants her art to be.

"Surprise!" Vola cheers.

"Happy Mom and Mama's Day!"

Vola is an artist like her mama

and she can build things like her mom.

William notices Vola's family
looks different than his family too.
He swims home to talk to his mom.

"I noticed our family doesn't look like every other fishy's," William says to his mom. Baby Shark's, Hank's, and Vola's families are all different.

His mom tells him that all families
are unique.

Families are different.

It's something to celebrate!

"It's our love that brought us together," William's mom says. "And the Manta Family Whirlpool Swirl!"

William's mom gives him a big hug.

"It doesn't matter what we look like.

All that matters is that

I'm your mom and you're my son."

"I love you, Mom!" William says.

"Come on, I have something
for you!"

29

"Surprise!" he cheers.

"Happy Mother's Day, Mom!"

William and his mom dance together.

William wrote a special song
for her.

He and his friends sing it together.

All the families join in and sing.

"We're all families of fishies,

and our love's as big as

the seven seas."

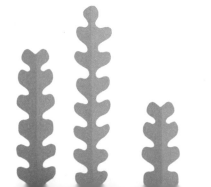